Put Beginning Readers on the Right Track with
ALL ABOARD READING™

The All Aboard Reading series is especially designed for beginning readers. Written by noted authors and illustrated in full color, these are books that children really want to read—books to excite their imagination, expand their interests, make them laugh, and support their feelings. With fiction and nonfiction stories that are high interest and curriculum-related, All Aboard Reading books offer something for every young reader. And with four different reading levels, the All Aboard Reading series lets you choose which books are most appropriate for your children and their growing abilities.

Picture Readers
Picture Readers have super-simple texts, with many nouns appearing as rebus pictures. At the end of each book are 24 flash cards—on one side is a rebus picture; on the other side is the written-out word.

Station Stop 1
Station Stop 1 books are best for children who have just begun to read. Simple words and big type make these early reading experiences more comfortable. Picture clues help children to figure out the words on the page. Lots of repetition throughout the text helps children to predict the next word or phrase—an essential step in developing word recognition.

Station Stop 2
Station Stop 2 books are written specifically for children who are reading with help. Short sentences make it easier for early readers to understand what they are reading. Simple plots and simple dialogue help children with reading comprehension.

Station Stop 3
Station Stop 3 books are perfect for children who are reading alone. With longer text and harder words, these books appeal to children who have mastered basic reading skills. More complex stories captivate children who are ready for more challenging books.

In addition to All Aboard Reading books, look for All Aboard Math Readers™ (fiction stories that teach math concepts children are learning in school) and All Aboard Science Readers™ (nonfiction books that explore the most fascinating science topics in age-appropriate language).

All Aboard for happy reading!

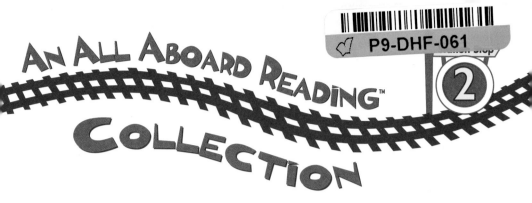

An All Aboard Reading™ Collection

2

School Rules!

Grosset & Dunlap

The All Aboard Station Stop 2 Collection:
SCHOOL RULES! published in 2003.

Published by Grosset & Dunlap, a division of Penguin Young Readers Group, 345 Hudson Street, New York, NY, 10014.
ALL ABOARD READING and GROSSET & DUNLAP are trademarks of Penguin Group (USA) Inc. Published simultaneously in Canada. Printed in the U.S.A.

ISBN: 0-448-43336-2   A B C D E F G H I J

AN ALL ABOARD READING™ COLLECTION

Station Stop 2

School Rules!

By Bonnie Bader, Cathy East Dubowski and Mark Dubowski,
Gail Herman, and Joan Holub

Illustrated by Cathy East Dubowski and Mark Dubowski,
Bryan Hendrix, Joan Holub, and Stacy Peterson

Grosset & Dunlap
New York

Table
of
Contents

100 MONSTERS
IN MY SCHOOL

By Bonnie Bader
Illustrated by Bryan Hendrix

There are 100 monsters in my school.

There are 25 witches in my reading group.

They can fly through any book they read.

There are 25 ghosts in the lunchroom.

They love eating "scream cheese"

and jelly sandwiches.

There are 25 vampires in my gym class.

They can swing from the highest places.

There are 25 werewolves

in my music class.

My ears hurt when they sing.

Usually, I like school.

I like to read books.

I read slowly.

I like to eat lunch.

I eat peanut-butter-

and-jelly sandwiches.

I like gym class.

I can walk

on the balance beam.

I like music.

I sing very softly, but very high.

But the worst day of school
is the 100th day of school.
All the monsters in my school
love the 100th day of school.
I do not.

Our teacher, Ms. Vampira,

told us that we each have to bring

in 100 things for show-and-tell.

What should I bring in?

100 books? Too heavy.

100 thumbtacks? Too sharp.

"I want tomorrow to be spook-tacular!"

Ms. Vampira said.

All the monsters in my class were excited.

I was not.

"I do not want to go to school tomorrow,"
I told my mother at dinner.

"Why not?" she asked. "Are you sick?"

I shook my head no.

"I don't have anything to bring in for
the 100th day of school," I said.

My mom smiled.

"I'm not worried about you, Jane,"
she said.

"You will think of something.
Just use your head."

The next morning,

I walked to school slowly.

Wendy Witchman saw me

in the school yard.

She was dressed in all black,

as usual.

"What did you bring in for the

100th day of school?" she asked me.

I did not answer her.

"Well, I brought in

something very special.

But I'm not telling you what it is."

Wendy flashed me a smile

and flew away.

Sally Spookster was behind me in line.
"What did you bring in for the 100ᵗʰ day
of school?" she whispered.

I felt a chill run down my spine.

Sally was nice.

She was very, very quiet.

But she was nice.

"I did not know what to bring in,"

I told her.

"You will think of something, Jane,"

Sally told me.

We walked inside the classroom.

"Welcome to the 100ᵗʰ day of school!"

Ms. Vampira said.

"We will start our show-and-tell now,"

she said.

I slid down in my seat.

I did not want Ms. Vampira

to call on me.

I had nothing to show.

Or tell.

"Victor Fangly," Ms. Vampira said.

"Why don't you go first?"

Victor stood up and smiled.

All of his front teeth were missing.

Except for his two fangs.

They were very sharp and very pointy.

"I have brought in my fang collection,"
Victor said with a smile.

He held up a bunch of little bags.

"I have 10 cat fangs,

and 10 dog fangs," he began.

"I have 10 monkey fangs

and 10 alligator fangs.

I have 10 fangs from my grandma.

And 10 fangs from my grandpa.

They don't need their fangs anymore."

Everyone in the class laughed.

"I have 10 of my brother's baby fangs.

And 10 of my sister's baby fangs."

"I have 10 fangs
that I found
at the beach.

And I have 10 fangs
that I'm going to leave
for the Fang Fairy."

At my house, the Tooth Fairy comes,

but I didn't want to say anything.

"That makes 100 fangs in all!" Victor said.

"Thank you, Victor!" Ms. Vampira said.

"That was fang-tastic!

Who will be next?" Ms. Vampira asked.

I slid down further in my seat.

"Pick me! Pick me!" Wally Wolfson called.

"Okay," Ms. Vampira said.

"I will show you 100 of my best howls,"

Wally said.

"Aooo!" Wally howled.

"That's 1."

"Aooo!" Wally howled even louder.

I put my hands over my ears.

It was a long way to 100 howls!

Ms. Vampira called on lots of other kids.

Sally Spookster told 100 spooky stories.

That took a long time.

And I got scared 100 times.

Bob Batty showed us his bat collection.

He had 50 fruit bats.

And he had 50 vampire bats.

That was a lot of bats.

I was glad they were in cages!

Wendy Witchman brought in
her cat collection.

"I have 20 cat stuffed animals,"
Wendy said.

She put the toys in front of
Ms. Vampira's desk.

"I have 20 cat keychains."

"I have 20 cat T-shirts.

I have 20 cat earrings.

That is really 10 pairs of earrings.

And I have 20 kitties."

Wendy opened up a big case.

20 little kittens came out

and looked at the class.

"Achoo!" I sneezed.

"Meow! Meow!" cried the cats.

I must have scared them.

The cats ran all over the room.

"My things!" Wendy cried.

"My 100 things!"

We raced around the room finding

all of Wendy's 100 things.

Finally, everything was found.

"Sorry," I told Wendy.

I handed her back the last kitty.

I tried not to sneeze.

Wendy took the kitty from me.

But she did not say a word.

Just then the lunch bell rang.

"Okay, class," Ms. Vampira said.

"We will finish our show-and-tell
after lunch."

Good.

That would give me some time to think.

I sat down at my lunch table.

But I did not feel like eating.

"Don't worry, Jane," Sally whispered.

"You'll think of something to show."

I put my head down on the table.

"Here," Sally said.

"These will make you feel better."

She handed me 5 marshmallow ghosts.

And 5 marshmallow mice.

Victor tried to cheer me up, too.

He gave me 5 bubble-gum bats.

And 5 bubble-gum owls.

Soon lots of kids at the lunch table
had given me something.

I had 5
gummy worms.

And 5

gummy bears.

I had 5

licorice witches.

And 5

licorice brooms.

I had 5

taffy pumpkins.

And 5

taffy apples.

I had 5

cherry eyeballs.

And 5

cherry lips.

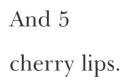

 I had 5

vanilla stars.

And 5

vanilla moons.

 I had 5

lemon goblins.

And 5

lemon skeletons.

 I had 5

strawberry spiders.

And 5

strawberry snakes.

 And I had 5

chocolate cats.

And 5

chocolate rats.

I looked at all the things in front of me.

All 100 things!

Just then, Wendy walked over to the table.

"Yum!" she said. "Mind if I share?"

She reached down and popped

5 chocolate cats into her mouth.

Now I was left with only 95!

The bell rang.

It was time to go back to class.

"Let's finish our show-and-tell,"

Ms. Vampira said.

"Jane Brain," she said. "It is your turn."

Oh, no! What was I going to do?

I stood up.

But I tripped over my lunch bag

and fell down!

The class howled.

My face turned red.

"Settle down, class," Ms. Vampira said.

"Jane, are you okay?"

"Y-yes," I said.

"Why don't you take a minute and get
yourself together," Ms. Vampira told me.

"Glenda Specter, why don't you go next?"

I picked up my lunch bag

and peeked inside.

My mom had packed me a good lunch.

Too bad I didn't eat it.

I had a tuna sandwich.

I had an apple.

I had 5 chocolate cookies.

Wait! 5 cookies?

I was ready for show-and-tell.

"Thanks to my friends,

I have 100 treats

for the 100th day of school,"

I told the class.

"10 marshmallow treats.

10 bubble-gum treats.

10 gummy treats.

10 licorice treats.

10 taffy treats.

10 cherry treats.

10 vanilla treats.

10 lemon treats.

10 strawberry treats.

And 10 chocolate treats!"

I smiled at the class.

"And since there are 25 people in the class,
we each get 4 treats!" I said.

"Hurray!" the class shouted.

"I can't wait to sink my teeth into them!"
Ms. Vampira said.

The 100th day of school
didn't turn out so badly after all!

Pen Pals

By Joan Holub

"The names of your new pen pals
are in this box,"
Mr. Perry told the class.
Daisy was excited.
She was going to write letters
to her pen pal.
And her pen pal was going
to write back.

Daisy chose a name from the box.

"Becky Benson," she read.

"Who did you get?"

asked Booger Wilcox.

His real name was Wally.

But only Mr. Perry called him that.

Daisy told Booger

the name of her new pen pal.

"Who did you get?" asked Daisy.

"I am not telling," Booger said.

That was just like Booger!

He drove Daisy nuts.

Lisa ran over to them.

"Guess what!" she said.

"My pen pal is named Lisa too!"

Booger waggled his fingers.

"Oooooh," he said in a ghost voice.

"I bet she is your evil twin."

Lisa rolled her eyes.

"Yeah, right," she said.

Mr. Perry clapped his hands.

"Okay, class," he said.

"Quiet down.

Now get ready, get set, WRITE!"

Daisy wrote a letter.

Dear Becky,

My name is Daisy James.
I go to Pine Tree School.
I am in second grade.
My teacher is Mr. Perry.
I like to draw. Do you?

From,
Daisy

She drew daisies on the letter.

It looked cool.

A week later,

letters came from the pen pals.

Daisy read hers.

Dear Daisy,
My name is A....

This is what it said.

Dear Daisy,

My name is not Becky.
It is Bucky.
I am a boy.
I am in second grade
at Willow Tree School.
My teacher is Ms. Flakes.
I like to draw too.

From,
Bucky

P.S. I do not want a girl
for my pen pal.

"My pen pal can do three

cartwheels in a row!" shouted Kyla.

"My pen pal has a treehouse," yelled Ned.

"My pen pal Kirby is

the best hockey player

in his school!" shouted Booger.

It was not fair!

Everyone had a good pen pal but Daisy.

Daisy went to Mr. Perry's desk.

"Can I trade pen pals?" she asked.

Mr. Perry shook his head.
"That might hurt your
pen pal's feelings," he said.
"Try a little harder to make friends."
"Okay," said Daisy.
What else could she do?

Daisy stomped over to the book nook.

Lisa was there.

"My pen pal has red hair," she told Daisy.

"And glasses—just like me."

Booger stopped feeding the hamster.

"Ah-hah!" he butted in.

"I told you she was your evil twin."

"She is not," said Lisa.

But she did not sound so sure.

Lisa looked a little worried.

But Daisy had pen pal

problems of her own.

She went back to her desk.

She wrote another letter.

Dear Bucky,

I do not want a boy
for my pen pal.
But Mr. Perry says
I have to keep you.
We have to write about pets.
My pet is a rat.
His name is Scout.
He runs around my neck.

From,
Daisy

She did not draw

daisies on this letter.

Just for fun,

Daisy got out more paper.

She drew a picture of her rat, Scout.

But she did not send it to Bucky.

It was too good for him.

Daisy took her letter

to the mailbox.

When she got back,

her rat picture was gone!

It was not on the floor.

Where was it?

After recess,

Daisy saw Booger.

He was snooping at her desk.

Oh, no!

He was reading the letter from Bucky!

Booger smiled.

"You said your pen pal

was a girl," he said.

"But Bucky is a boy."

"Snoop!"

shouted Daisy.

Daisy clobbered him on the back.

Mr. Perry was not around.

That was lucky.

Mr. Perry did not like snooping.

But he did not like clobbering either.

The next week,

more pen pal letters came.

Lisa read hers.

"Oh, no!" she wailed.

"My pen pal has a cat."

"Lots of people have cats," said Daisy.

"A calico cat.

Like I have," said Lisa.

Booger hooted.

"The evil twin strikes again!" he said.

Daisy made a mean face at Booger.

She put her arm around Lisa.

Daisy read Bucky's letter at lunchtime.

Dear Daisy,

I am sending back your
stinky rat picture.
I do not look like a rat.
Here is what I think you
look like—my dog, Beanie.
We have to write
about the summer.
I went to the beach.
I got a ton of shells.

From,
Bucky

P.S. Here is what rhymes
with Daisy—Crazy.

Bucky

How did Bucky get her rat picture?

Daisy had not put Bucky's name on it.

Someone else had done that.

And that same someone

had put it in the mailbox.

Daisy bet she knew who it was.

After lunch, Daisy wrote back to Bucky.

Dear Bucky,

Here is what I did last summer.
I went to see some caves.
People lived in them a long time ago.
Some of their arrows and stuff
are still there.
Somebody else wrote your name
on my rat picture.
Not me.

From,
Daisy

P.S. Here is what rhymes
with Bucky—Yucky!

P.P.S. I do not look like a dog.

Daisy put her letter in the mailbox.

She wished that it was summer right now.

Then she would not have to write

to her dumb pen pal.

On Thursday mornings,

the whole class went to the art room.

Daisy loved art class best of all.

Today the art teacher told the class,

"Draw your favorite animal."

Daisy opened her markers.

"Are you going to draw another rat?"

asked Booger.

"I knew it!" said Daisy.

"<u>You</u> took my rat picture

and mailed it to Bucky.

You are the biggest rat of all!"

87

Booger did not look sorry.

"Daisy has a boyfriend,"

he started singing.

Daisy pretended that Booger was not there.

Booger began making kissy noises.

But Daisy kept pretending that

she could not hear him.

Booger could not stand it!

The very next day, Mr. Perry

passed out new pen pal letters.

The pen pals had sent school pictures.

Bucky was right.

He did not look like a rat.

Daisy read his letter.

Dear Daisy,

Those caves sounded cool —
even cooler than the beach.
You write good letters.
You draw good pictures.
Maybe it is not so bad
that you are my pen pal.

Your pen pal,
Bucky

"Look at my pen pal's picture," said Lisa.

Lisa's pen pal had red hair and glasses.

But she did not look like Lisa.

"She looks nice," said Daisy.

"Not like an evil twin at all."

Lisa nodded.

They both stared at Booger.

But Booger was looking
at his pen pal's picture.
He was shaking his head.
"Let me see," said Daisy.
"No!" said Booger.

Too late!

Daisy had already seen.

"Ha-ha! Booger's pen pal is a <u>girl</u>!"

shouted Daisy.

"Kirby is a girl!"

Daisy and Lisa smiled big smiles.

95

"Want to trade?" Booger asked Daisy.

"Then you would have a girl.

And I could have a boy."

Daisy shook her head.

"No way!

I would not stick Bucky with you."

On Saturday, Daisy wrote back to Bucky.

Dear Bucky,

Wally Wilcox is Kirby's pen pal.
He did not know Kirby was a girl.
I did not know you were a boy.
Funny, huh?
Wally wanted to trade pen pals.
But I said no.
I am glad you are my pen pal.

Your pen pal,
Daisy

Uh-oh. She almost forgot.

At the bottom of her letter,

Daisy added one last thing—

am gla...

Your pen pal,
Daisy

P.S. Be sure and tell Kirby that Wally's real name is Booger.

100

Pirate School

By Cathy East Dubowski
and Mark Dubowski

Pete's family

was a lot like other families.

Every morning

his mom and dad got breakfast.

His baby sister watched

Jolly Roger's Neighborhood.

And Pete rowed the bus

to school.

Pete went to school

on a ship.

The ship was called

P.S. 1.

The P.S. stood for

PIRATE SCHOOL!

Pete learned to add

by adding up gold coins.

He learned to subtract
by making classmates
walk the plank!

The kids at P.S. 1

were as hard as nails.

And so were the rules.

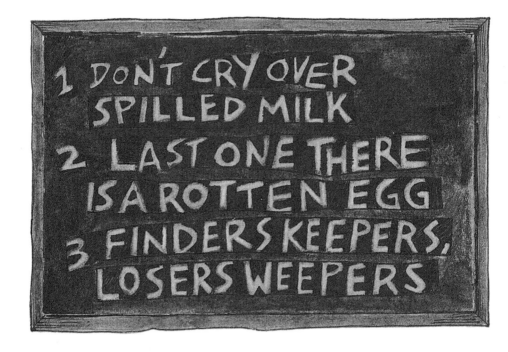

1 DON'T CRY OVER
SPILLED MILK
2 LAST ONE THERE
IS A ROTTEN EGG
3 FINDERS KEEPERS,
LOSERS WEEPERS

Pete liked everything

about Pirate School.

Well, almost everything . . .

He hated Gregory Grimes the 13th!

(The kids called him Grimy.)

And Grimy hated Pete right back!

"You're too little
to lift the anchor!"
said Grimy.
"You're too big
to get through the hatch!"
said Pete.

"You little shrimp!" shouted Grimy.

"You big whale!" shouted Pete.

"STOP THAT!" yelled their teacher
Captain Bones.

Captain Bones did not like
kids to call each other names.
"Act like big pirates," he said.
"And <u>fight</u> it out!"

So they did.

Who won?

"I did!" said Grimy.

"No I did!" said Pete.

At Pirate School

the biggest day of the year

was Treasure Hunt Day.

Captain Bones held up a map.

"The treasure is hidden here,"

he said.

"X marks the spot.

Find it,

and you get to keep it."

"Finders keepers!" hissed Grimy.

"Losers weepers!" snapped Pete.

All the kids rowed

to the shores of Skull Island.

Pete and Grimy fought all the way.

"I'm going to find

the treasure first!" said Grimy.

"No, I'm going to find it first!"

said Pete.

On Skull Island the class split up.

They all ran off to find

the X that marked the spot.

Pete looked high.

Pete looked low.

"I've got to find that X

before Grimy," he thought.

Pete went deeper and deeper

into the woods.

"That X could be anywhere,"

he said.

So he looked everywhere!

No luck!
At last he sat
down to think.
Suddenly he felt as if
someone was watching him.
Slowly he turned around. . . .

"The X!" he cried.

"I found the X!

It looks just like the one on the map!"

"Forget it!" somebody yelled.

"I found it first!"

It was Grimy!
They had found the X
at the same time!
It was on the side
of an old ship.
"Scram!" said Grimy.
"The treasure is mine!"

"You want to fight about it?"

said Pete.

So they did.

Captain Bones would have been proud.

CRASH!

Pete and Grimy

fell through the rotted deck!

Down, down they went

into the dark!

Pete and Grimy hit bottom.

It was dark and wet and smelly.

Slowly their eyes

got used to the dark.

"L-look!" said Pete.

It was the treasure!

"We found it!" they cheered.

But then they stopped cheering.

They looked around.

There were no steps.

No ladder.

No rope. No door.

They were trapped!

"We'll never get out!"

cried Grimy.

"We'll starve to death.

By the time they find us,

we'll be a pile of bones!"

Pete and Grimy sat down

on the treasure

and waited to die.

"Hey, Pete," said Grimy.

"Are you scared?"

Pete nodded.

"Well, I'm more scared

than you!" said Grimy.

"No, I'm more scared

than you!" said Pete.

But before they could fight it out,

Pete got an idea.

First he got Grimy to help him

turn the treasure chest on its side.

Then he made Grimy

stand on top of the chest.

Then Pete stood on top of Grimy.

"Give me a boost!" Pete cried.

Grimy did.

Pete hit the deck with a thud.

"Ouch!" he said. "I made it!"

He grabbed a rope.

"Tie this to the treasure!"

he called down to Grimy.

Pete turned the crank

and pulled the treasure up.

Pete couldn't wait

to see what was inside.

He opened the chest.

"Wow!" he cried.

He had never seen so much

treasure!

"And it's mine!" he shouted.

"All mine!"

"Hey, Pete!" called Grimy.

"What about ME?"

Pete looked down

into the big, dark hole.

Suddenly he had a terrible idea.

"I could just leave him there,"

he thought.

"He'd be a pile of bones.

And I would have all the treasure!"

"Aw, shellfish!" said Pete.

"I just can't do it!

If it weren't for Grimy's help,

I'd still be stuck down there, too."

So he threw down the rope

and pulled Grimy out.

"Thanks, mate," said Grimy.

"I was scared you were

going to leave me."

"No, I couldn't do that," said Pete.

"But don't tell Captain Bones

that I saved you.

He'd be mad!"

Together they carried the treasure

back to their boat.

Back at the ship

all the kids cheered.

But Captain Bones frowned.

"We have never had a tie before,"

he said.

"I guess there is only
one thing to do.
Act like big pirates
and fight it out!"

But Pete and Grimy had a better idea.

"We want to split it," said Pete.

"Fifty-fifty," said Grimy.

"Even Steven," said Pete.

So they did.

And that worked out great—

until there was just one coin left.

Pete and Grimy looked at it.

Everyone looked at Pete and Grimy.

What would they do now?

Were they going to fight it out?

No!

They flipped for it!

I've Got the Back-to-School
Blues

By Gail Herman

Illustrated by Stacy Peterson

When Annie and Katie and

Laura were five,

they were in the same kindergarten class.

When they were six,

they were in the same first-grade class.

But now they were seven.

Katie and Laura were going to be

in the same second-grade class.

But not Annie.

Annie sat on her steps

and looked at her best friends.

They were right next to her,

like they had always been.

But second grade would change everything.

"Tomorrow is the first day of school,"

Annie told her friends.

"You two will be together.

And I'll be with . . ."

Annie got the class list.

Sure, she knew some of the kids.

There was Martin.

He hardly ever spoke.

Then there was Eric.

He was okay.

But he only liked dinosaurs
and baseball.

And there were Sara and Emma.

All they did was play <u>together</u>.

"I'll be with nobody!" Annie said.

"Come on, Annie," said Katie.

"Second grade is not the end

of the world.

Our classroom will be next door."

"That's right," Laura agreed.

"And you can visit.

You know our teacher Mr. Carr.

He likes kids to stop by and say hi."

Sure, Annie knew Mr. Carr.

Everyone wanted him for a teacher.

His class played games, sang songs,

and went on great field trips.

And her teacher?

She was new.

Annie didn't know one thing about her.

MS
TOADY

"What's your teacher's name again?"

Katie asked.

Annie frowned.

Katie knew the teacher's name.

She just wanted to hear it again.

"Ms. Toady," Annie finally said.

Katie and Laura laughed.

Second grade might not be
the end of the world,
Annie thought.
But it sure felt that way.

When Laura and Katie left,

Annie stayed outside.

Maybe if she didn't move,

tomorrow would never come.

School would never start.

"Hey you!" called a girl riding by

on her bike.

It was Jenna,

another second-grader.

Annie hoped she would keep going.

Jenna could be awfully mean.

Screech! Jenna stopped.

"I know you have Ms. Toady,"

Jenna sang in a loud voice.

"Toady, Toady, Toady.

Hopping in the roady."

Jenna laughed.

"I heard she's the meanest teacher ever.

And she's just like her name.

She eats flies.

She has warts.

And she doesn't walk.

She hops."

Screech! Jenna took off.

Annie didn't believe all that frog stuff.

Not really.

But what if Ms. Toady was

the meanest teacher ever?

166

Annie was so upset,

she jumped up to run inside.

All at once, she stopped.

"A moving truck," she said.

A new family was moving in,

just down the block.

There could be someone her age.

Maybe someone in her class.

So when Ms. Toady did something mean,

they could talk about it.

Maybe even laugh about it.

Annie walked closer.

She peered at the furniture

and clothes.

No kids' stuff.

Not even baby things.

FRAGILE

GLASS

Then a woman came out.

She smiled at Annie.

"Hello," she said.

"Hello," said Annie.

"Annie?" her mom called from

the house.

"Where are you?

Dinner is ready."

Annie turned to go. *Meow!*

A cat ran through her legs,

and down the street.

"Oh, no!" the woman cried. "Puffball!"

"I'll get her!" said Annie.

In a flash, she scooped up the cat.

"Here," she told the woman.

"Thank you so much," said the woman.

"Your name is Annie?"

Annie nodded.

"I'm—"

Just then, a second cat ran the other way.

"Sorry! Got to go!" the woman said.

"Annie!" her mom called louder.

"Come in right now!"

Annie waved to the woman.

She seemed nice.

If she had kids,

they would be nice, too.

But all the woman had were cats.

Nothing ever worked out right!

That night, Annie tossed and turned.

She hardly slept at all.

She kept thinking about school.

About second grade

with mean Ms. Toady—

and no friends in class!

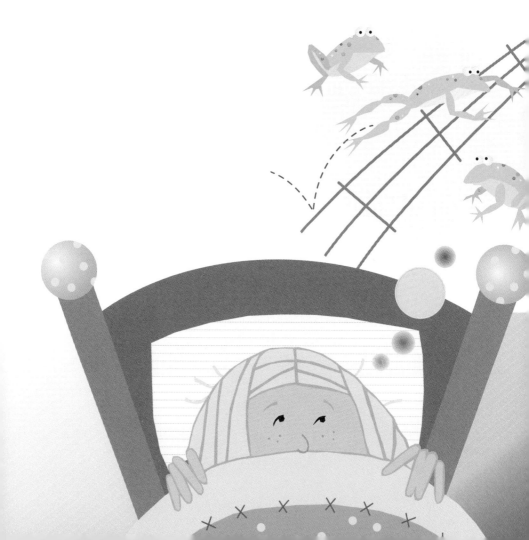

At breakfast, Annie tried to eat.

But she had a big lump in her throat.

It was hard to swallow.

Her mom gave her a hug.

"I know you are nervous about school,"
she said.

"Try not to worry.

You'll make new friends.

And Laura and Katie will still be your
best friends."

Annie nodded, but she didn't believe it.

Katie and Laura would talk about

their class.

People she didn't know.

They would walk home—just the two

of them.

Pretty soon, they'd forget all about her.

Annie sighed.

If only she didn't have Ms. Toady!

A little later,

Annie walked into her classroom.

She looked all around.

Emma was talking to Sara.

Max was talking to Martin.

Everyone was talking to somebody.

Everyone but Annie.

All at once, she gasped.

A mean-looking woman bent over a desk.

She had green skin.

Well, almost green skin.

And big bulging eyes.

Well, really big eyes.

Ms. Toady!

The woman stacked some papers.

Then she turned to go.

She was only bringing notices!

She wasn't Ms. Toady after all.

OH no!

And now Annie could see someone else.

Someone behind that woman.

It was her new neighbor, from down

the block.

The one with the runaway cats.

And she was coming over!

"Hello," the woman said.

"I'm Ms. Toady.

We didn't get to talk the other day.

I'm so glad you are in my class."

"To tell the truth," she went on.

"I feel a little nervous.

After all, I'm new to the neighborhood,

and to school.

Maybe you can help me?

Show me around?"

Annie smiled.

All along, she'd been feeling

sorry for herself.

But poor Ms. Toady.

She must feel really alone.

"Sure," Annie said. "I am happy to help."

After school, Annie walked outside

and grinned.

Katie and Laura were waiting!

They didn't forget her.

"Hi!" Annie said.

Then she saw Ms. Toady.

"Good-bye, Ms. Toady," she called out.

This time, no one laughed.

"Your teacher said hello

to me in the hall," Katie said.

"She seems really nice."

Annie smiled. "She is."

"I'm going to love school this year!"

Abby Cadabra, Super Speller

By Joan Holub

Abby Cadabra was a super speller.

She could spell short words

like C-A-T and T-O-A-D.

And she could spell longer words

like S-P-I-D-E-R, too.

None of the other little witches

at witch school were as good.

Then one day, at thirteen o'clock,

a new little witch showed up.

Ms. Poof clapped her hands.
"Class," she said,
"this is Wanda Cassandra."
Wanda sat down
next to Abby.

Abby saw a pin on Wanda's hat.

"That's my spelling medal,"

Wanda bragged.

"I was the best speller at

my old school."

Abby rolled her eyes.

Wanda was going to be

<u>second</u> best around here.

"That reminds me," said Ms. Poof.

"We are having a spelling bee tomorrow!"

The little witches gulped.

Spelling bees at witch school

were extra hard.

First each little witch

had to spell a word.

Then she had to say

why it was spelled that way.

And <u>then</u> she had to use the word

in a magic spell!

Ms. Poof said,

"The best speller will win

a very special prize."

She got something out of the closet.

"It is a rocket-powered flying broom!"

Abby gazed at the broom
with love in her eyes.

But Wanda said,

"Don't count your brooms

before they zoom.

Because I am going to win.

Just wait and see."

Abby did not want to wait and see.

She had to find out how good

Wanda's spelling was <u>now</u>.

So after school,

she followed Wanda home.

She peeked in Wanda's window.

Wanda was working on her spelling.

"W-I-N-N-I-N-G," Wanda spelled.

Then she said the rule:

"If the last letter is a consonant,

double it so there are two

before you add a suffix

that starts with A, E, I, O, or U.

Win—double N,

add I-N-G—

make me the winning witch

of the school spelling bee."

Zzzzap! A big bee appeared.

It sprinkled magic dust

all over Wanda.

The magic dust would make her win.

That was cheating!

Abby jumped through the window.

"No fair!" she yelled at Wanda.

Wanda spun around.

"Snoop!" she shouted at Abby.

"C-H-E-A-T-E-R,"

Abby spell-yelled.

"Sometimes two letters

make just one sound,

like in words where

the letters CH are found.

Cheater, cheater,

I declare!

I see Wanda's underwear!"

A breeze blew around Wanda.

It blew until her long undies showed.

"I bet you can't win

fair and square!" Abby said.

Wanda frowned.

"Can, too!" she said.

"I'll undo my winning spell.

And we'll just see who wins!"

So Wanda called off her spell.

And Abby zipped home

to work on her spelling.

At school the next day,

the spelling bee began first thing.

An hour later, only two witches

were still standing—

Abby and Wanda.

Both of them had spelled

every word correctly so far.

Ms. Poof called on Abby.

"Spell FROGS," she said.

Abby spelled, "F-R-O-G-S."

She said the rule:

"Add S to most words

to show two or more.

One frog, two frogs,

three frogs, four!"

Then she cast her magic spell.

Hippity! Ploppity! Hop!

Four frogs appeared.

They leaped all over Wanda.

Wanda screamed.

Abby smiled.

Her spell had worked!

Ms. Poof turned to Wanda.

"Spell FRIEND," she told her.

Wanda spelled,

"F-R-I-E-N-D.

I before E

except after C,

or when pronounced 'ay'

as in NEIGHBOR and WEIGH."

Now came her magic spell.

"Little furry black bat,

do you want to be my friend?

Then fly around that witch's hat

and land upon its end."

Itchy! Twitchy!

A cute little bat flew into the room.

It sat on the tip of Abby's hat.

Everyone clapped.

Abby felt silly.

Back and forth

and back and forth.

Abby and Wanda spelled

all morning.

Then Ms. Poof said to Abby,

"Spell BROOMSTICK."

Gadzooks! thought Abby.

A compound word!

Abby wiggled her ears

and thought hard.

Then she took a deep breath.

"B-R-O-O-M-S-T-I-K,"

she spelled.

Ms. Poof stopped Abby.

"I'm sorry," she said kindly.

"But that is not correct.

Wanda, can you spell it?"

Oh no! thought Abby.

Now Wanda was going to win!

Wanda twitched her nose

and thought hard.

"B-R-U-M-S-T-I-C-K,"

she spelled.

Ms. Poof stopped Wanda, too.

"That is not right either,"

Ms. Poof said.

"So who won?" asked the little witches.

"We'll see," said Ms. Poof.

"Let's go to the next word . . ."

Just then,

Abby thought of something.

"Wait!" she cried.

She turned to Wanda.

"Come on," Abby whispered.

"I've got an idea."

Abby and Wanda

hopped on their brooms

and flew out of the classroom.

The other little witches

ran to the window to watch.

In the air,

Abby yelled over to Wanda.

"I know how to spell BROOM,"

she said.

Wanda yelled back,

"And I know how to spell STICK!"

Abby nodded.

"Let's put them together,"

said Abby.

In big sky writing,

Abby spelled:

Wanda spelled:

Then they pushed their words
closer together.

Ta-dah!

Now they spelled one big word:

BROOMSTICK.

Abby and Wanda landed their brooms

in front of the classroom window.

Together, they shouted:

"B-R-O-O-M-S-T-I-C-K!

Take two little words,

and stick them together with glue.

You'll get a compound word

that's completely new."

Then they shouted,

"Brooms for sweeping.

Broomsticks to fly.

Broomsticks! Broomsticks!

Rain from the sky!"

Bobble! Wobble! Boom!

There was thunder.

There was lightning.

And then, brand-new broomsticks

rained from the sky!

Ms. Poof smiled.

"Abby and Wanda, you both win.

You will share the prize.

You both earned it

with your super spelling

and your teamwork!"

And that was that.

Wanda flew the prize broomstick

on Mondays and Tuesdays.

She flew in zigzag lines

all around outer space.

Abby flew the broomstick
on Wednesdays and Thursdays.
She made loop-the-loops
around the moon.

And on Fridays,

Abby and Wanda shared.

Heckle, speckle,

piffity, poof.

This story's done,

and here's the proof—

THE END